Sad,

Sad

William

The Netherlands
KINDERJURY
Prize
1996

For a free color catalog describing Gareth Stevens Publishing's list of high-quality books
and multimedia programs, call 1-800-542-2595 (USA) or 1-800-461-9120 (Canada).
Gareth Stevens Publishing's Fax: (414) 225-0377.
See our catalog, too, on the World Wide Web: http://gsinc.com

Library of Congress Cataloging-in-Publication Data
Spee, Gitte.
[Willem is verdrietig. English]
Sad, sad William / by Gitte Spee.
p. cm.
Summary: William, a big bear, feels far from beautiful and different from everyone else,
until his friends convince him he does have a talent to be proud of and that makes him special.
ISBN 0-8368-1607-2 (lib. bdg.)
[1. Self-esteem–Fiction. 2. Individuality–Fiction. 3. Bears–Fiction.] I. Title
PZ7.S7416Sad 1996
[Fic]–dc20 95-52871

First published in North America in 1996 by
Gareth Stevens Publishing
1555 North RiverCenter Drive, Suite 201
Milwaukee, Wisconsin 53212 USA

Original edition published in 1995 by Uitgeverij Zwijsen Algemeen B.V.,
Gasthuisring 58, 5041 DT Tilburg, Postbus 805, 5000 AV Tilburg, the Netherlands.
Text and illustrations © 1995 by Gitte Spee.

Printed in the United States

1 2 3 4 5 6 7 8 9 99 98 97 96

Sad, Sad William

Gitte Spee

Gareth Stevens Publishing
MILWAUKEE

William woke up one morning with a sigh.
He'd had a bad dream. Everyone in his dream was
smarter than he was, or could run faster, or could
do all kinds of clever things that he could not.

Slowly, William forced himself out of bed.
He shuffled into the bathroom. "Aargh!" he cried,
catching sight of himself in the mirror. "I'm not
only *not* clever, but I'm big and ugly, too!"

"What am I to do?" William whispered to himself.
"I'm going to stay home forever," he decided.
"I'm never going anywhere again!"

Sad, sad William wouldn't even let his friends
into his house. He didn't open the door for
Betsy and Bert, his very best friends.
And when they tapped on the window,
William pretended not to be home.
So they left, and William was all alone.

William stayed home all day, feeling sad and lonely.
By evening, he was hungry. So he put on
sunglasses and wrapped himself in a blanket.
He snuck out the door and into the woods
to find something to eat. Surely no one
would recognize him in this disguise.

In the woods, William found some berries.
Suddenly, Betsy and Bert came running by,
but they did not know who he was.
"Have you seen our friend William?" they asked.
"He's a big fat bear, and we can't find him
anywhere!" But the "stranger" just
stood up, howled, and ran away.

"That proves it," sobbed William through his tears.
"I *am* big. And I bet they think I'm stupid and ugly, too."
Sad, sad William ran all the way home.

Betsy and Bert followed, keeping out of sight.
They watched the "stranger" go into William's house.
They were horrified. What if the stranger
were a burglar or a kidnapper?
Their friend could be in serious danger!

No one answered when they pounded
on William's door. So they found an
open window and climbed inside.

Betsy and Bert were coming to the rescue!

Betsy and Bert rushed into the living room.
Bert put up his fists, and Betsy pulled the blanket
away from the stranger. It was William!

"Go away. I don't want anyone to see me,"
said William, and he began to cry.

But Betsy and Bert would not leave.
So William told his friends about
his dream, and about how big
and ugly and stupid he was.

"Oh, William," said Betsy. "You *are* big.
Bears are supposed to be big. And you're
handsome, too! Your fur is silky and such a
lovely color, and your nose is the shiniest
and most beautiful nose in the world."

"But you are so *clever*," said William,
"and I'm so *stupid*. I can't do anything well."

"Maybe *you* can't do the things that *I* do well," said Betsy,
"but that is because *you* are a bear and *I* am a rabbit.
I can do the things that *rabbits* can do well, and
you can do the things that *bears* can do well.
I am not better than you, just different,"
said Betsy. "And you're *not* stupid!"

"I bet we can think of lots of things that
you could be great at!" said Betsy.
So the three friends thought for a moment.
"I've got one!" Bert shouted.
"Bears are good at learning tricks.
That's quite a talent!"

William was a little clumsy at first.
He made a few slips . . .

but with practice,
and hard work . . .

and a little help from his
friends, William started to
feel better about himself.

William was not perfect. But, then, who is?
The important thing was that he was
trying hard and making progress.
Betsy and Bert were so happy for him!
And William felt like such a lucky bear.

William practiced and practiced, making the
best of the talent he was blessed with.
Then, one day he decided to invite some friends
over for a performance. Betsy and Bert
helped him get ready for the big day.

William sent out invitations
to everyone he knew,
and he practiced for hours
and hours every day.

At last, the big day arrived.
Everyone enjoyed being together.
They gave William loud bursts of applause
as he showed off his unique talents.
William smiled. Deep inside, he knew that he
was just as special as anyone — and just a
little bit, just a wonderful bit, different!